THIS BOOK BELONGS TO

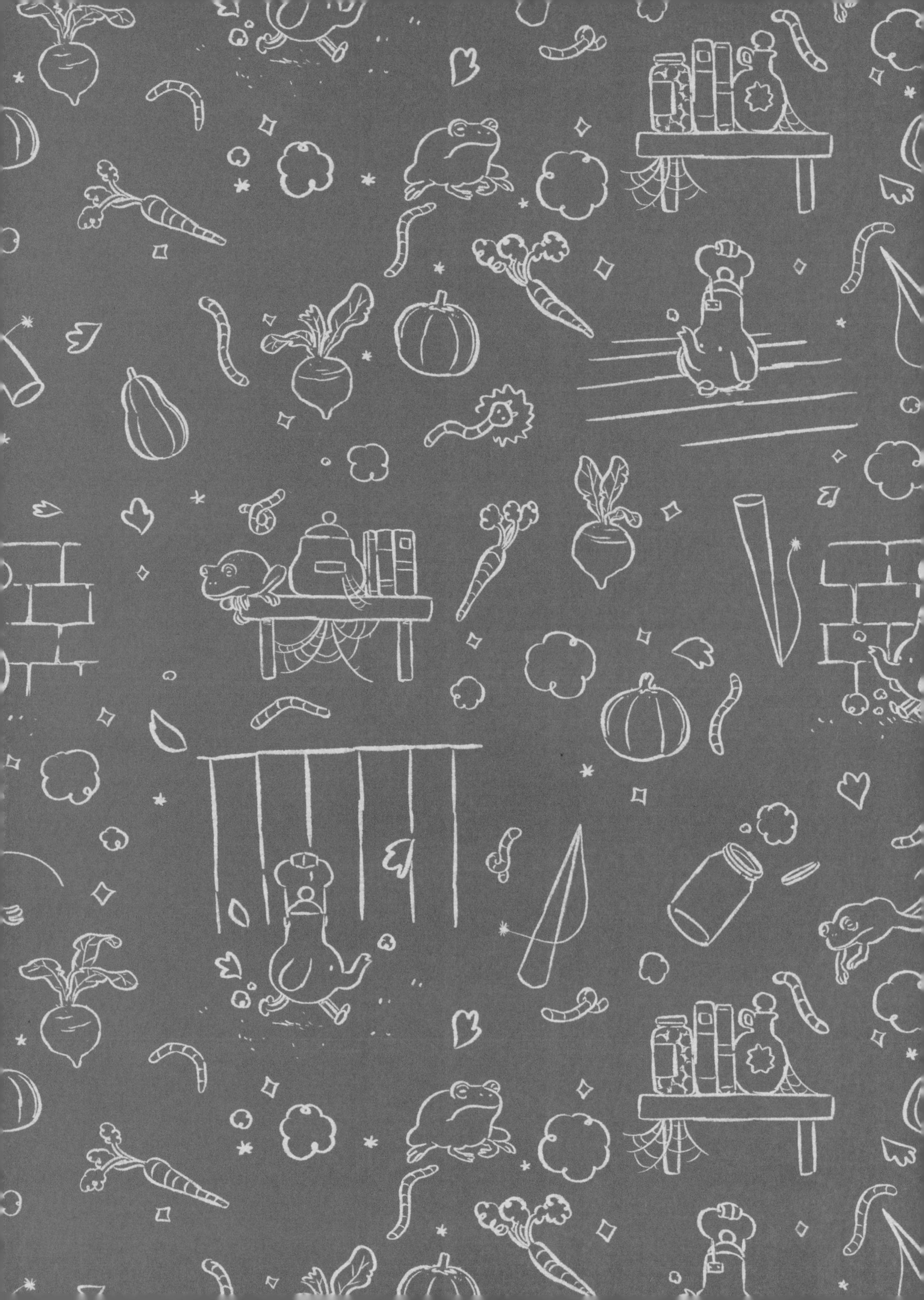

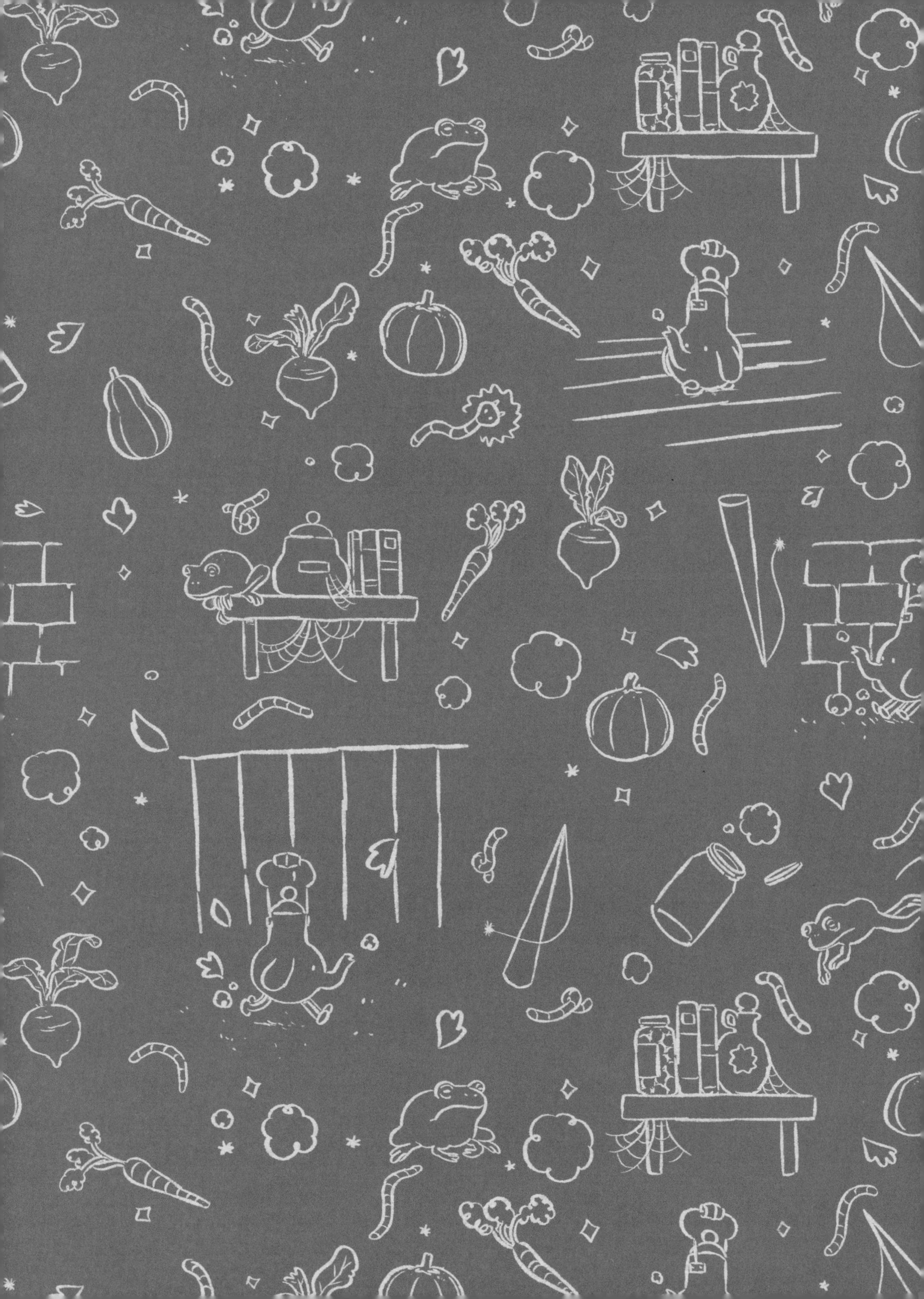

For Mum, Emma, Kelly,
and another Emma.

This edition published in 2022 by Flying Eye Books,
an imprint of Nobrow Ltd. 27 Westgate Street, London, E8 3RL.

Text and illustrations © Isaac Lenkiewicz.

Isaac Lenkiewicz has asserted his right under the Copyright, Designs and
Patents Act, 1988, to be identified as the Author and Illustrator of this Work.

1 3 5 7 9 10 8 6 4 2

Published in the US by Nobrow (US) Inc.

Printed in Poland on FSC® assured paper.

ISBN: 978-1-83874-014-6

www.flyingeyebooks.com

Isaac Lenkiewicz

ALCATOE
AND THE
TURNIP CHILD

Flying Eye Books

Plum Woods is an ordinary stretch of woodland, at first glance. But if you spent a night amongst the trees, you'd soon run into one of the hundreds of ghosts, goblins, and I expect even some of the curious knee-high folk. But there's one inhabitant of the woods who's even more mysterious.

Not an imp, a ghoul, nor a hob. The most reclusive
creature in all of Plum Woods is... me, Alcatoe.

I got into witchcraft when I was 54 years old and I haven't looked back since. It can help you solve all kinds of problems. For example, say one day you can't be bothered to get up and make a cup of tea. Just conjure yourself a kettle dog!

A regular cup of tea doesn't always cut it for me though. Being a witch opens you up to a world of delicious new tastes!

They were all out of milk, Stovetop. Can you believe that? We might have to lay low for a while – it wasn't easy getting this alternative.

CHILDREN'S TEARS

SUGAR

One evening I was pottering in my kitchen
working on something really special...

Can you guess what it is? A potion that turns your fingers into tentacles? A sandwich that blows your head up to twice its size?

Oh, relax. It's just jam buns. I was making them for the Plumtown Witches' Social Club.

That night there was a full harvest moon.

It was the perfect kind of night to take the chair out for a ride.

The Thirsty Toad was an old pub run by witches, for witches.

And on the first Thursday of each month, the witches living in the area gathered there to share spells and discuss other witchy business.

Goonwartha was the head of the Social Club. She placed great importance on having a public image that was the exact opposite of mine.

She absolutely adored her familiar, Big Mash, the brute hog.

We were there to discuss the Social Club's annual Harvest Feast.

After digging out an old hat from lost and found for me to wear, Goonwartha meticulously went through the plans for the event.

You see, some people reckon I was responsible for a rift between us witches and the non-witches of Plumtown. The townsfolk never really appreciated my youth club for worms, for instance. This event was meant to restore harmony.

But little did I know some local children had started to become a little too curious about me...

They shared stories about my antics. Like how the oldest child, Chris, had a run in with one of my overprotective blackberry bushes.

He told his friend Holly, who decided she wanted to be a witch when she grew up.

She told her sister, Emma, who was less keen on all things witchy, after the summer she ate one of my cursed fruit salads.

Those pesky children couldn't stop talking about me. Even on their way to school they were thinking about good old Alcatoe. And when they discovered my precious hat, all our fates were sealed.

Your dad has been a complete and utter donkey and forgotten to wake you up because he thinks it's Saturday already.

Did your gran just call your dad a donkey?

Yeah, that's what she calls him when he does something silly.

A hat!

It looks like a witch's hat.

Best not to wear it then, Holly. You might turn into a little witch yourself!

I think it IS a witch's hat. In fact, I saw Alcatoe wearing one just like it last night.

You actually saw her? That's so cool! I can see the funny coloured smoke coming from her chimney from my window and that's creepy enough.

Come on, we're going to be late. Let's cut through the allotments – it's ten minutes faster.

What if Mr Pokeweed is there?

Oh great, from the topic of one creep to another!

Mr Pokeweed was a nasty man. Never had someone's name been so suitably sharp and poky and weedy.

My dad says Mr Pokeweed's father was a goblin, so he's half goblin.

That's not true though, is it? Because your dad also said that Alcatoe drives around in a car that has arms and legs...

What a donkey...

He had an exceptionally strong sense of smell, which helped him back when he used to hunt foxes. He could sniff them out without a dog to help him.

Sniff sniff Mmmm hmm, smells about ready.

These days, thankfully, he only hunts vegetables.

A kingly turnip with a bumpy regal crown. Such character! *sniff*

Mr Pokeweed was fiercely territorial. He had caught the children taking that shortcut before.

That'll show you. My patch is not a shortcut!!! Next time it'll be the pumpkins I throw at you!

REJECTS (FOR THROWING)

BONK!

SCHOOL
I think I know how to get back at Pokeweed. Let's meet here after school. I'll have it fully figured out by then. Holly, keep a hold of that hat.
PLUMTOWN PRIMARY

Chris knew Mr Pokeweed only cared about vegetables and his own big head. They could get him back at next week's big event...

The harvest festival vegetable pageant!

We're going to beat his prize turnip. We'll grow one the size of his ego!

In a week? How is that going to work?

Witch magic.

PROPERTY OF ALCATOE. IF FOUND - RETURN IMMEDIATELY!

So that night after I'd left the Witches' Social Club meeting, I was paid a visit.

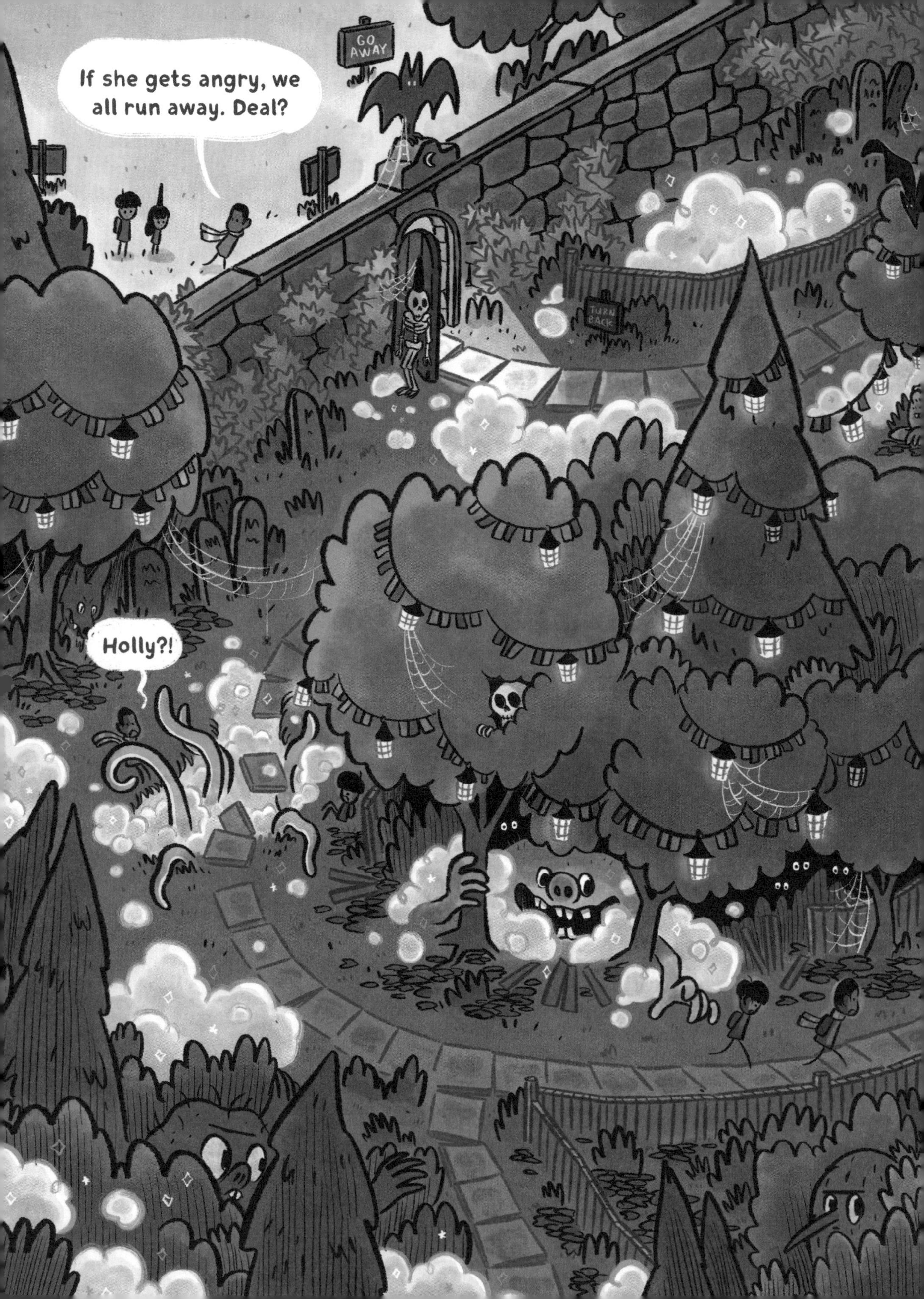

GO AWAY
If she gets angry, we all run away. Deal?
TURN BACK
Holly?!

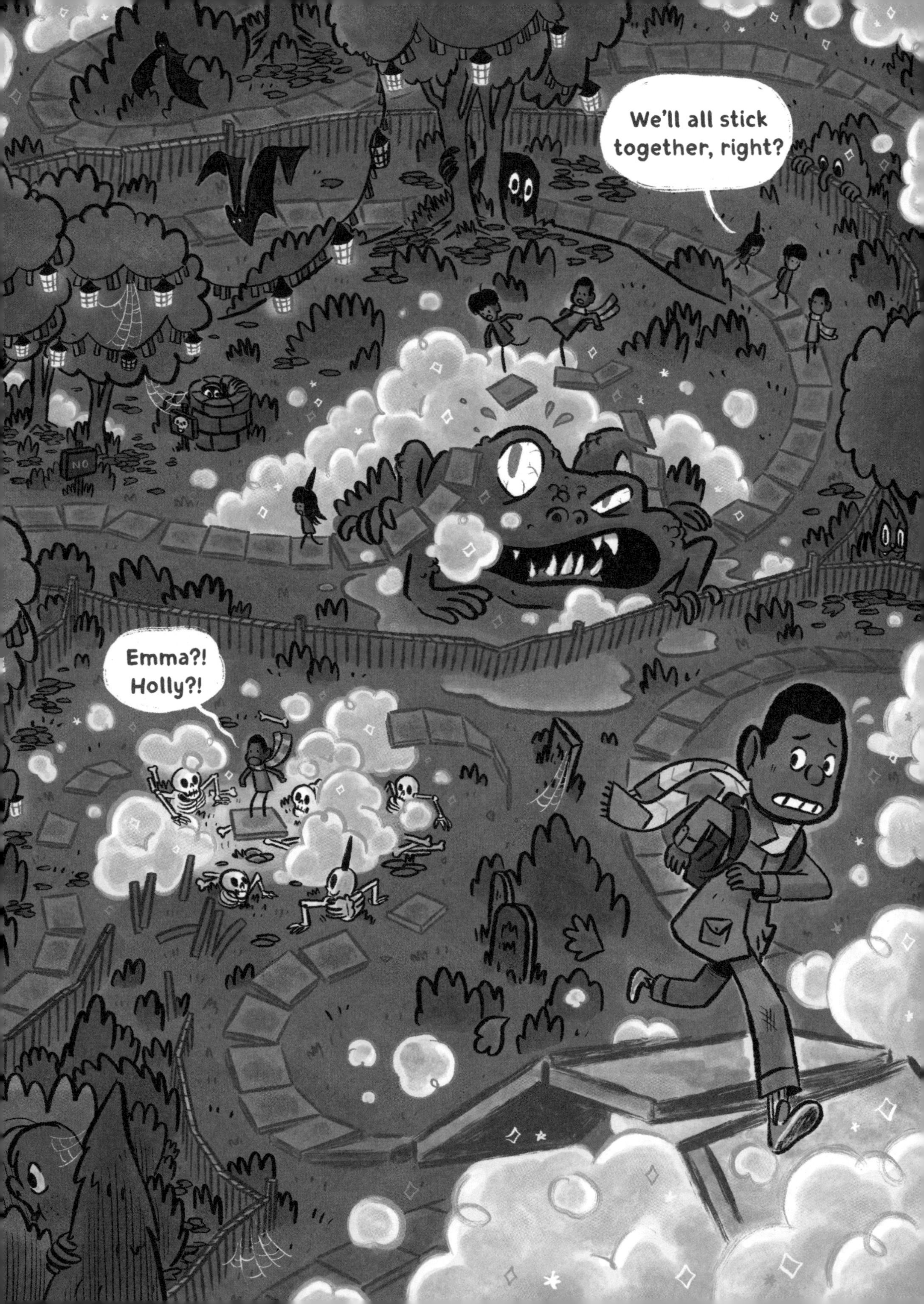
We'll all stick together, right?
Emma?! Holly?!
NO

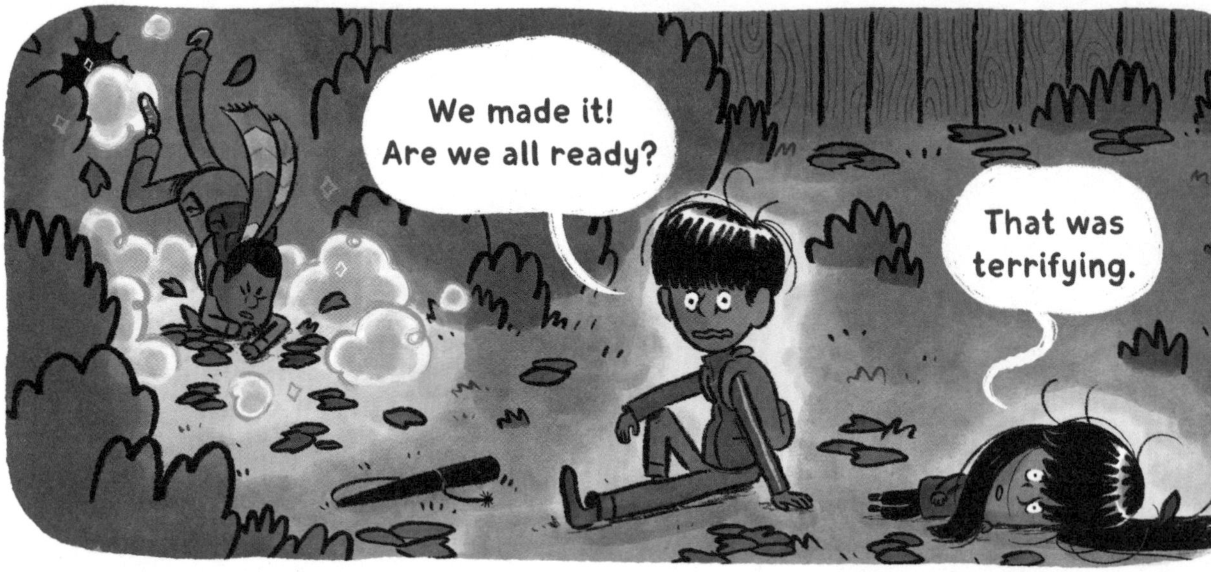
We made it!
Are we all ready?
That was terrifying.

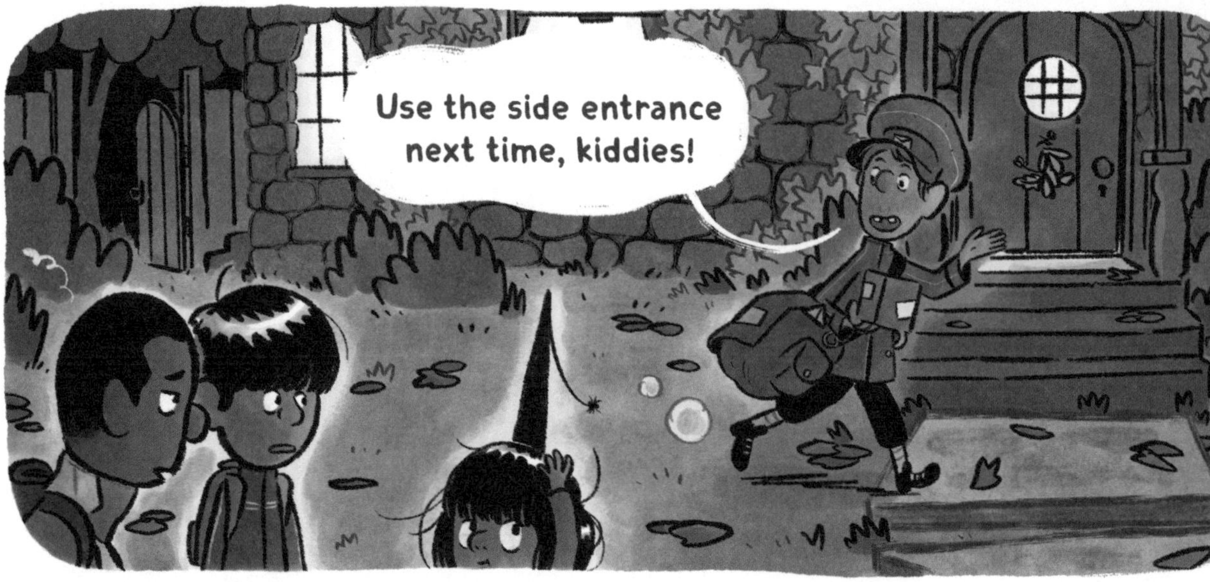
Use the side entrance next time, kiddies!

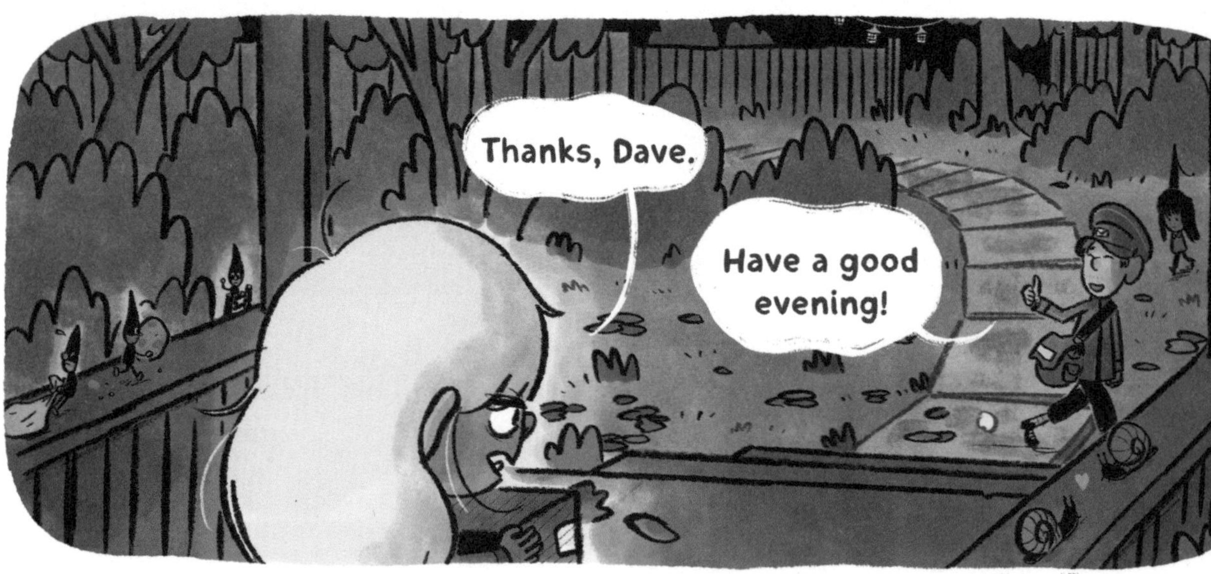
Thanks, Dave.
Have a good evening!

Excuse me, Ms Alcatoe. We found your hat. We were hoping you would help us if we returned it to you?

You will give me back my hat or I will make you into a new hat!

Please! We need your help to beat rotten Mr Pokeweed in the harvest festival vegetable pageant!

We need to grow a prize-winning turnip!

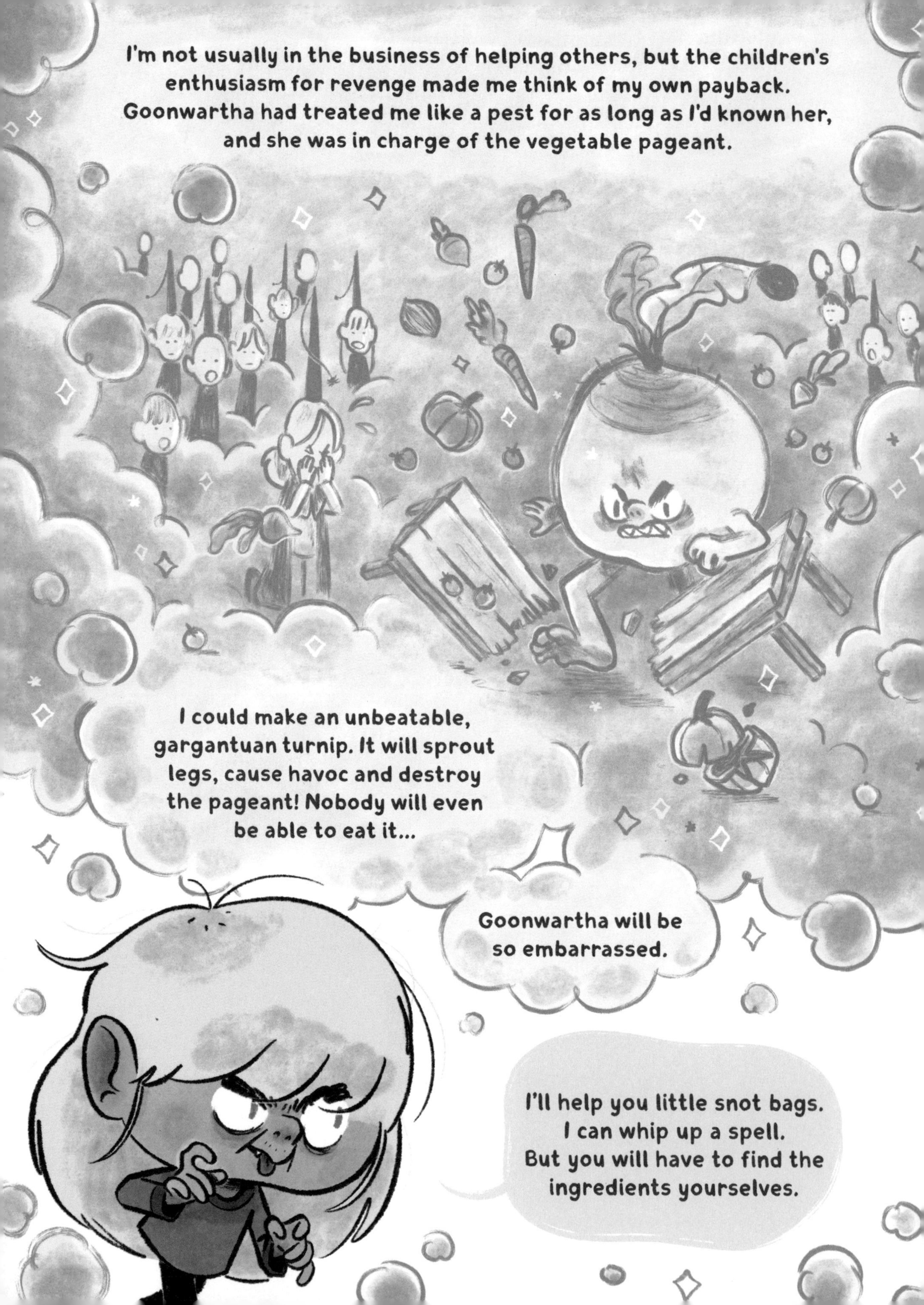
I'm not usually in the business of helping others, but the children's enthusiasm for revenge made me think of my own payback. Goonwartha had treated me like a pest for as long as I'd known her, and she was in charge of the vegetable pageant.
I could make an unbeatable, gargantuan turnip. It will sprout legs, cause havoc and destroy the pageant! Nobody will even be able to eat it...
Goonwartha will be so embarrassed.
I'll help you little snot bags. I can whip up a spell. But you will have to find the ingredients yourselves.

The children couldn't believe their luck. I was helping *them*, the smelly little things. And I couldn't wait to see the look on Goonwartha's face.

FIRST YOU MUST GO TO HOB'S BRIDGE. TAKE STOVETOP WITH YOU, SHE WILL SHOW YOU THE WAY (ALSO SHE NEEDS WALKIES). ONCE THERE YOU WILL NEED TO SING A SONG AS YOU CROSS — IN RETURN YOU WILL BE GIFTED A TURNIP SEED.

YOU MUST THEN WALK TO THE EXACT CENTRE OF PLUM WOODS AND COLLECT A HANDFUL OF SOIL.

THE REST IS PRETTY SIMPLE:

- THE TAIL HAIR OF A COPYCAT
- THE SNEEZE OF A DONKEY
- AND A CHOCOLATE BAR

Emma took it upon herself to cross the bridge, while Chris and Holly decided to gather the rest before meeting up to find the exact centre of Plum Woods.

Stovetop reminded Emma that she had to sing a song.

Please, please, please stop singing! People always come here, singing at the top of their lungs and I have no idea why.

Here, take this. I don't mean to be rude, but please go away and leave me in peace.

Let's go and get that chocolate bar.

Toot!

Oh dear, that was embarrassing.

I feel like we should have asked what a Copycat is, because I honestly have no idea.

Will it look like a normal cat? How will we know the difference?

COPYCAT!

32

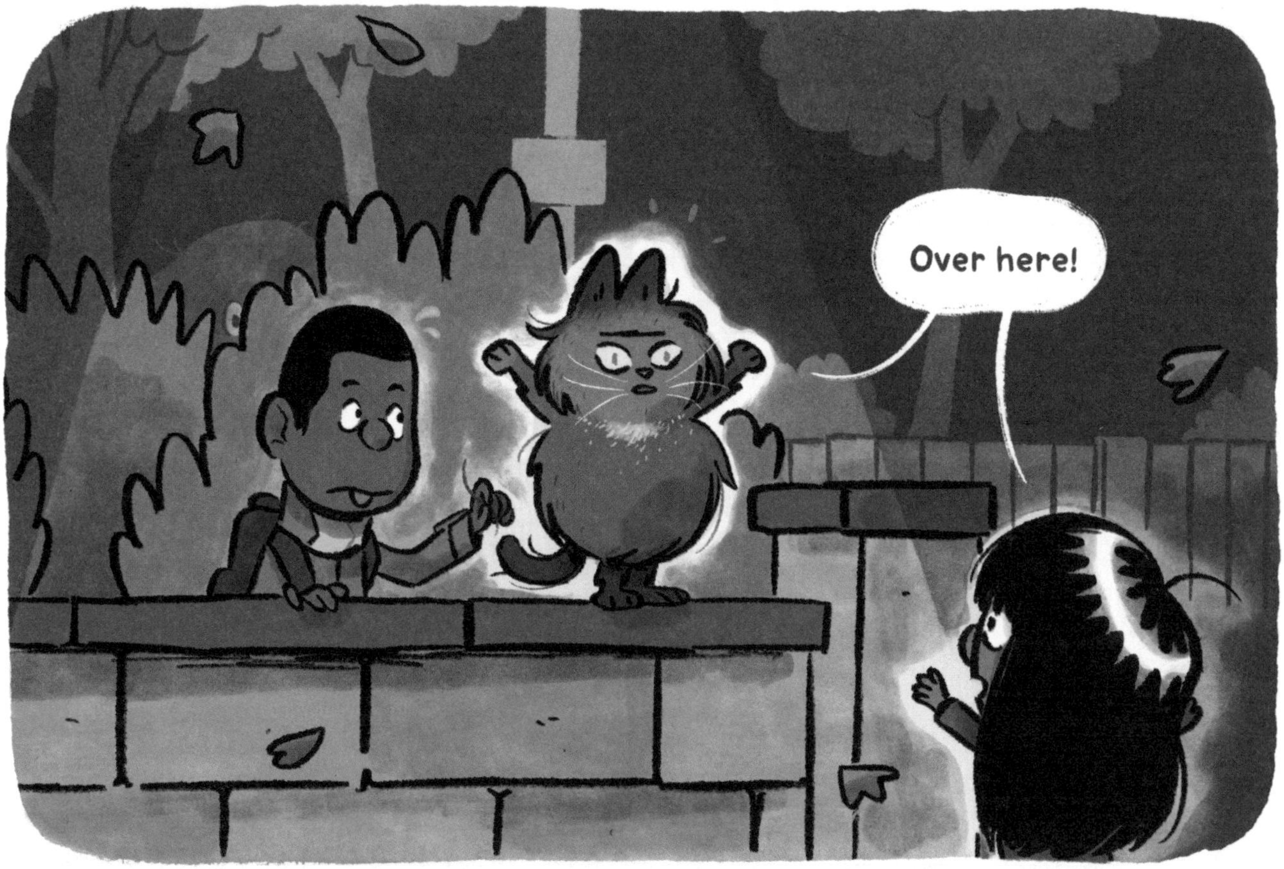
Over here!

The cat plucked a hair from Holly's head too and ran away. It's only fair I suppose.

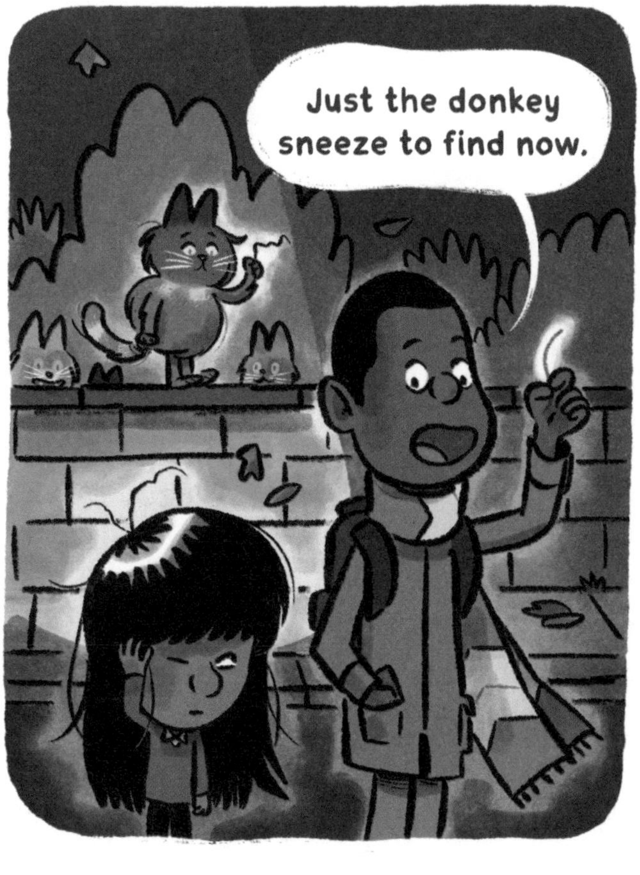
Just the donkey sneeze to find now.

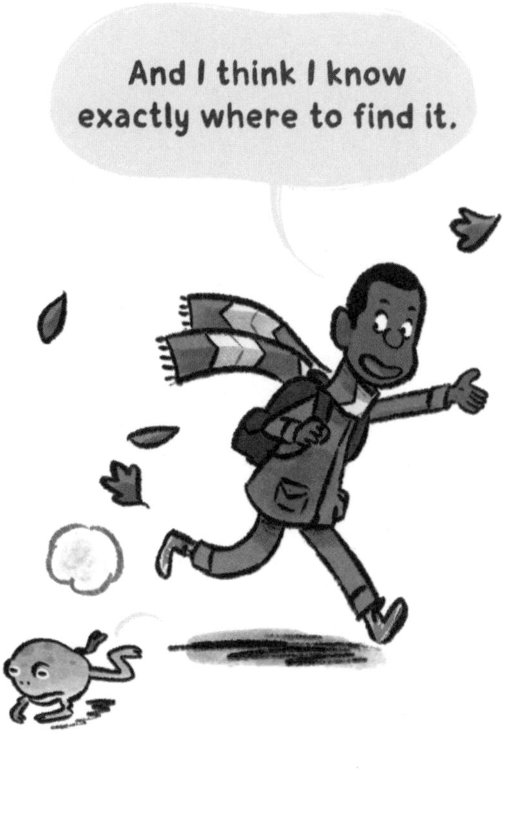
And I think I know exactly where to find it.

Chris had a great idea. He remembered how his grandma would call his dad a donkey when he did something silly.

Chris caught the snot and the "achoo!". It was really impressive.

I was happy enough with the ingredients and I began work on my first ever enchanted vegetable spell.

The children returned the next day to collect the spell.
They couldn't wait to be part of a witch's ritual.

What do you think it will look like? Is she going to give us a wand to wave?

Take this and bury it in the same spot in the centre of Plum Woods. Then add water from ten ice cubes that have been boiled and then chilled. Tomorrow you'll be ready to harvest your champion turnip.

Let's meet back here after breakfast tomorrow. We'll need to bring a wheelbarrow if it's as big as we hope.

The turnip was out, but wow, what an odd shape it was. Almost like...

...a child! You would have thought it was the same age as Holly, if you didn't know it was born just this minute.

The Turnip Child stretched out its arms and gave a wide yawn.

Hello... my name's Holly. This is my sister Emma and our friend Chris.

Let's speak to Alcatoe. The spell must have gone wrong and I'm sure she'll want to fix it.

The children came back to my house with the Turnip Child wrapped in Chris' scarf, so as not to draw attention.

They explained that, while they were pleased the turnip was astonishingly large, it was also astonishingly alive.

I have to say, I really outdid myself with this one. It was all part of my plan of course, but I didn't want them to know that.

What do you want me to do? I suppose I could make a jumbo turnip stew and we could start over...

So after teasing them a little, I convinced them to enter the pageant anyway.

You know what? I think this might even help you win.

The judges are going to love this little worm-nosed wonder. You can surprise them in the 'Special Attributes' round.

Perhaps this Turnip Child could jump up and do a dance. Ooh... or juggle swords?

Let's get some snacks and practise for the pageant.

Good idea.

STAY OUT.

The kids spent their time getting to know the Turnip Child.

Holly showed it how to cartwheel and the Turnip
Child showed her how to do a head stand.

Chris took the Turnip Child home, disguised as a harvest festival decoration.

It was the day of the vegetable pageant. The children felt fully prepared.

Remember, be as still as you can until the special attributes round. We want to surprise the judge!

VEGETABLE PAGEANT!

Mr Pokeweed was furious when he saw that the children had such an outstanding entry. He did everything he could to hold back a goblin growl.

Welcome everyone, to the Plumtown Harvest Vegetable Pageant! Before I forget, I'd like to thank all of the competitors for agreeing – as the pageant rules state – to donate their entries for tonight's grand harvest feast!

Oh no! We can't let them eat the Turnip Child. Let's leave – abort mission!

Now let's see what sets your entries apart from the rest! I want to see what's special. Show me what you've got!

SNAP!

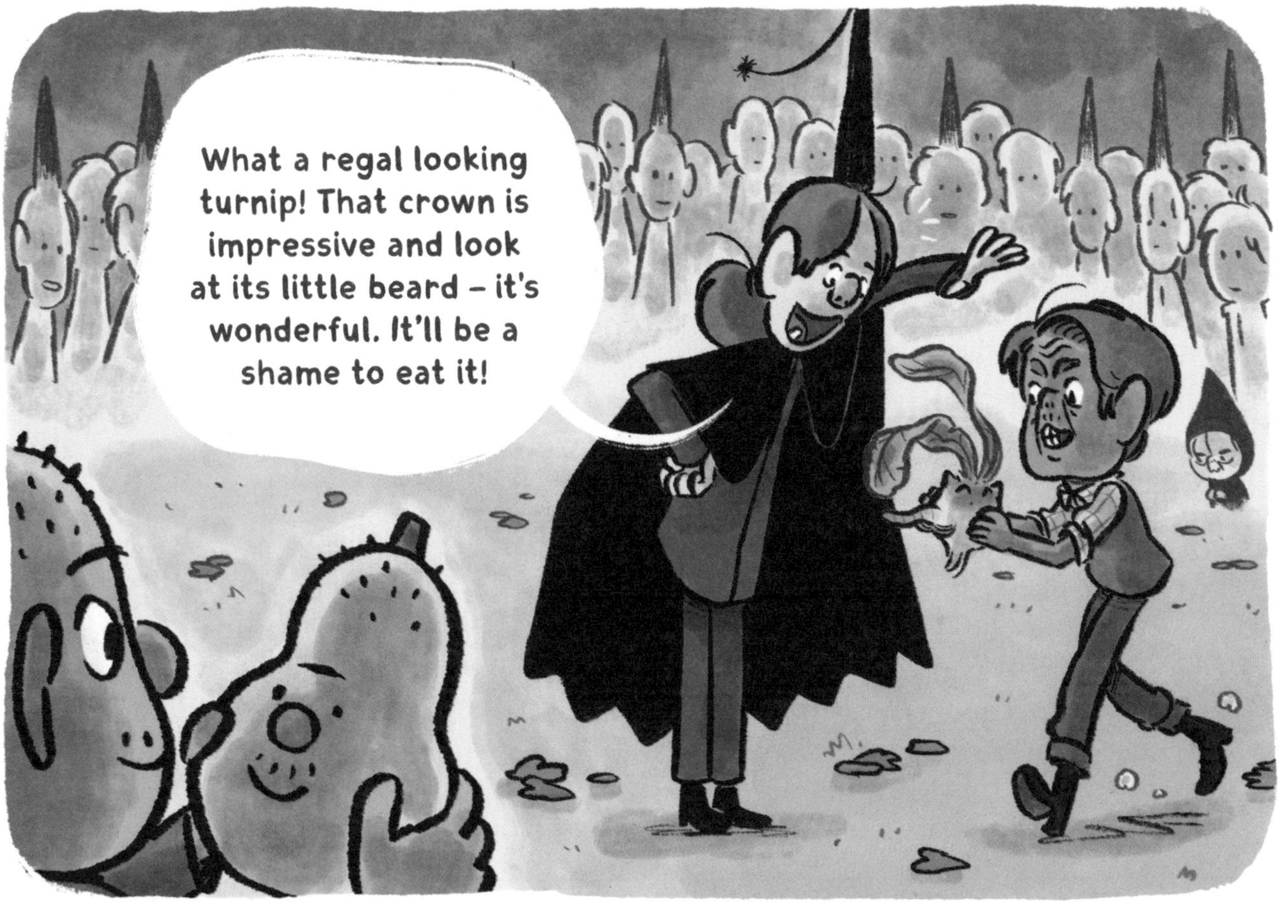
What a regal looking turnip! That crown is impressive and look at its little beard – it's wonderful. It'll be a shame to eat it!

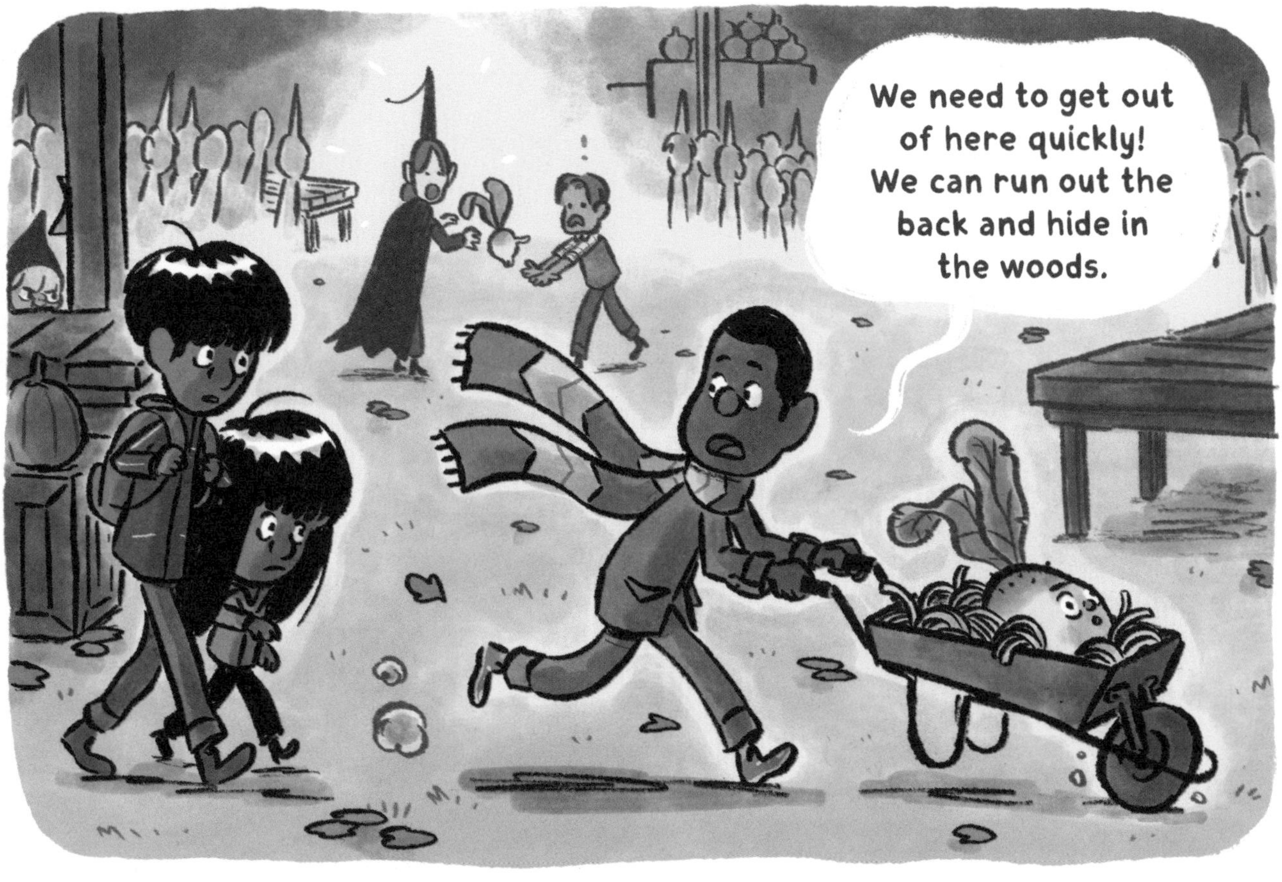
We need to get out of here quickly! We can run out the back and hide in the woods.

Wow! That is the largest turnip I've ever seen! I'm incredibly impressed, little ones. I especially look forward to preparing this gargantuan vegetable for the feast.

In fact, I don't even need to see anything else. I'm declaring this turnip the winner on the spot.

No!

I was thrilled. It went even better than I was expecting!

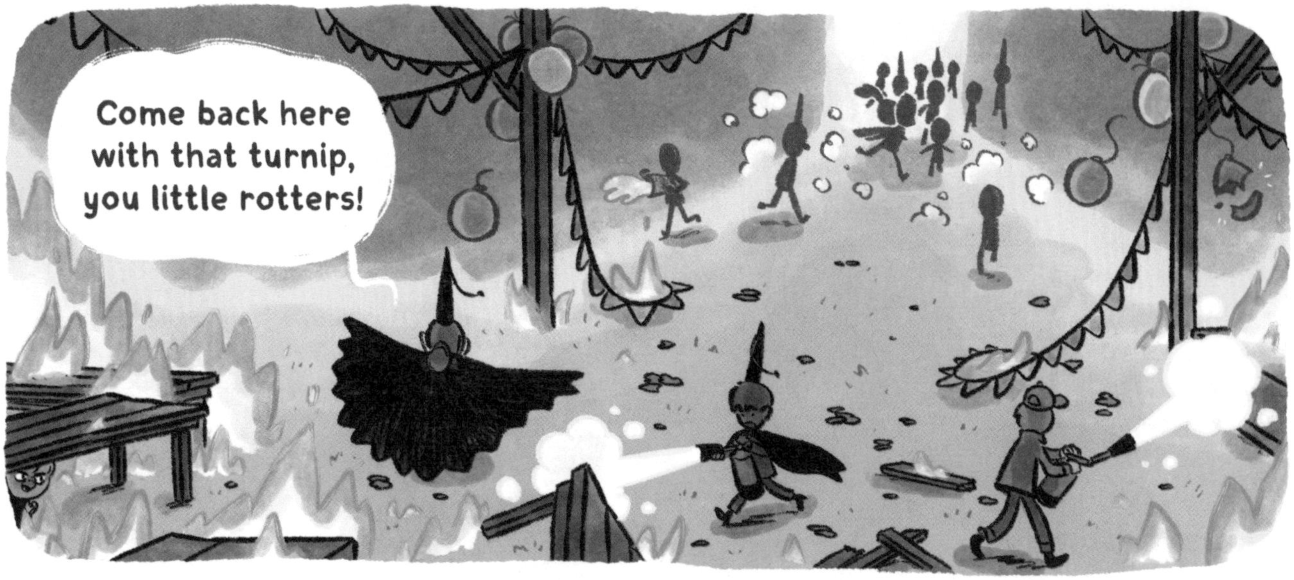
Come back here with that turnip, you little rotters!

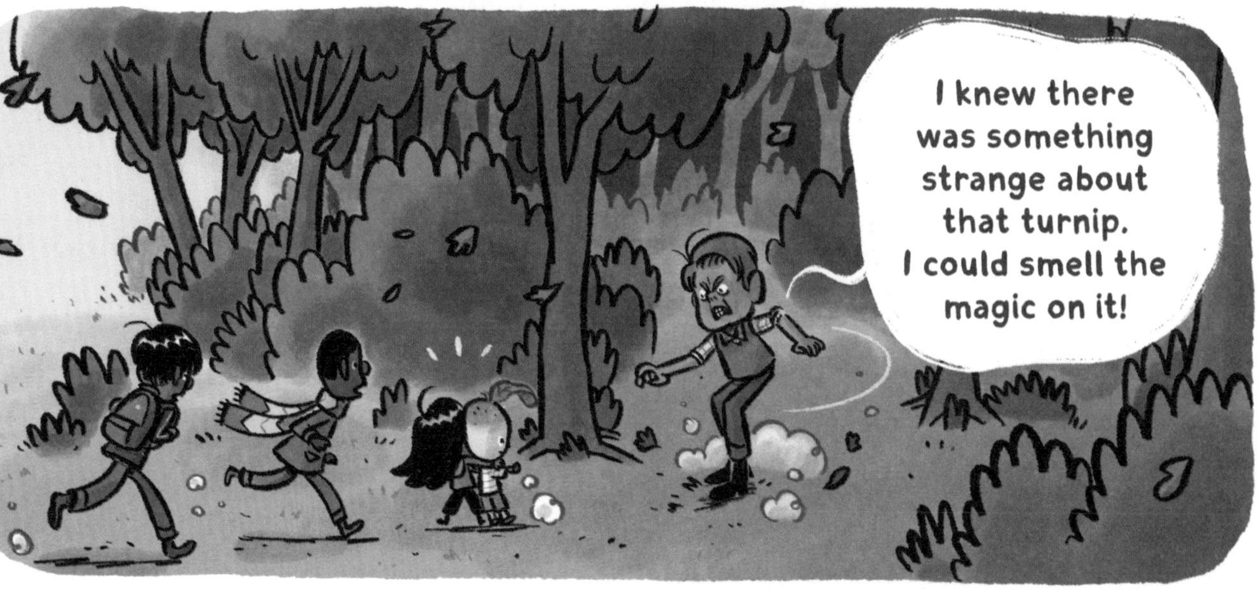
I knew there was something strange about that turnip. I could smell the magic on it!

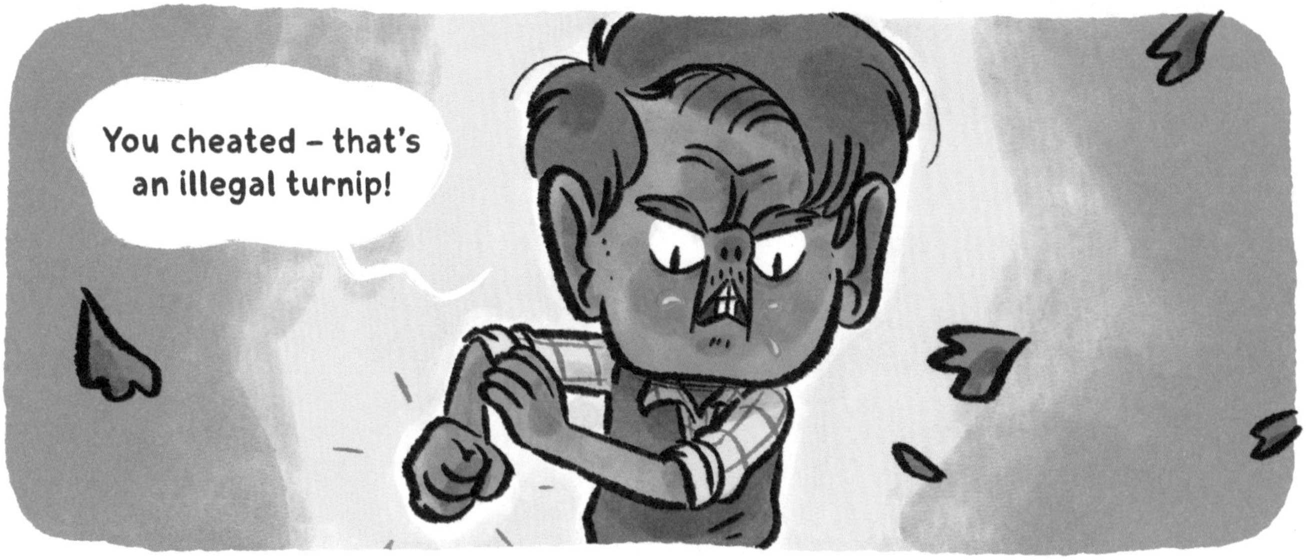
You cheated – that's an illegal turnip!

Goonwartha swept in and like a flash whipped her wand towards Mr Pokeweed, turning him into a pokey little weed.

She furiously explained that the Harvest Feast is a symbol of harmony between the witches and non-witches of Plumtown. It MUST go smoothly.

What is she going to do to the Turnip Child?

Didn't you listen to what Goonwartha just said? She's going to take the Turnip Child to the Harvest Feast.

Oh, that's not so bad!

No Holly, she's going to take it as food.

Oh no!

The kids rushed back to my house. It was up to me to save the day again.

Through Plum Woods we ran... drove? Well,
we sort of ran and drove through Plum Woods.

Listen up witches! We only have until this evening to cook a town's worth of food and get it out the door! Sisters, work your magic!

Hmm, how should I prepare the prize winner? Chop, oil and roast perhaps.

With plenty of garlic and of course rosemary... Mashy, get off my cape!

With a graceful entrance, I stopped Goonwartha just in the nick of time.

One tap of my wand and this turnip will be in pieces and on a roasting tin!

I don't think so!

HONK!

The children let out a big cheer. I had to cover my ears at the sound of elation.

I pointed out that Big Mash seemed to have taken a liking to the Turnip Child – and not in a food kind of way.

You don't know my hog better than me. Mash, stop being silly.

It looks like they're friends whether you like it or not, Goony. You wouldn't deprive Mash of something that makes him happy would you?

I really really couldn't. But how will we make up for the lack of food now?

The children ran to Mr Pokeweed's allotment and brought back his crate of rejected vegetables. There was no need for them to go to waste.

I was invited to the feast but I don't like big crowds. Anyway, I was far too busy.

Chris's grandma was more than happy to
welcome the Turnip Child into their home.

Goonwartha told the children that the Turnip
Child could visit Big Mash whenever they wanted.

Plum Woods is an ordinary stretch of woodland, at first glance.

It's home to hundreds of bats, a flower that resembles a cantankerous old man, and a child with the head of a turnip.

But if you look really closely, push through the thick branches and mind the stinging nettles, you might see the (admittedly rather kind and generous) people of Plumtown attending a grand Harvest Feast.

And last, but absolutely not least, one witch.
Who might even join the festival next year...

Isaac Lenkiewicz is an artist living in Plymouth, UK. He makes contemporary folk stories about things like witches, worms, ghosts, and goblins.

With a jumble of pop culture influences and nostalgic silliness, he aims to impress his childhood self.

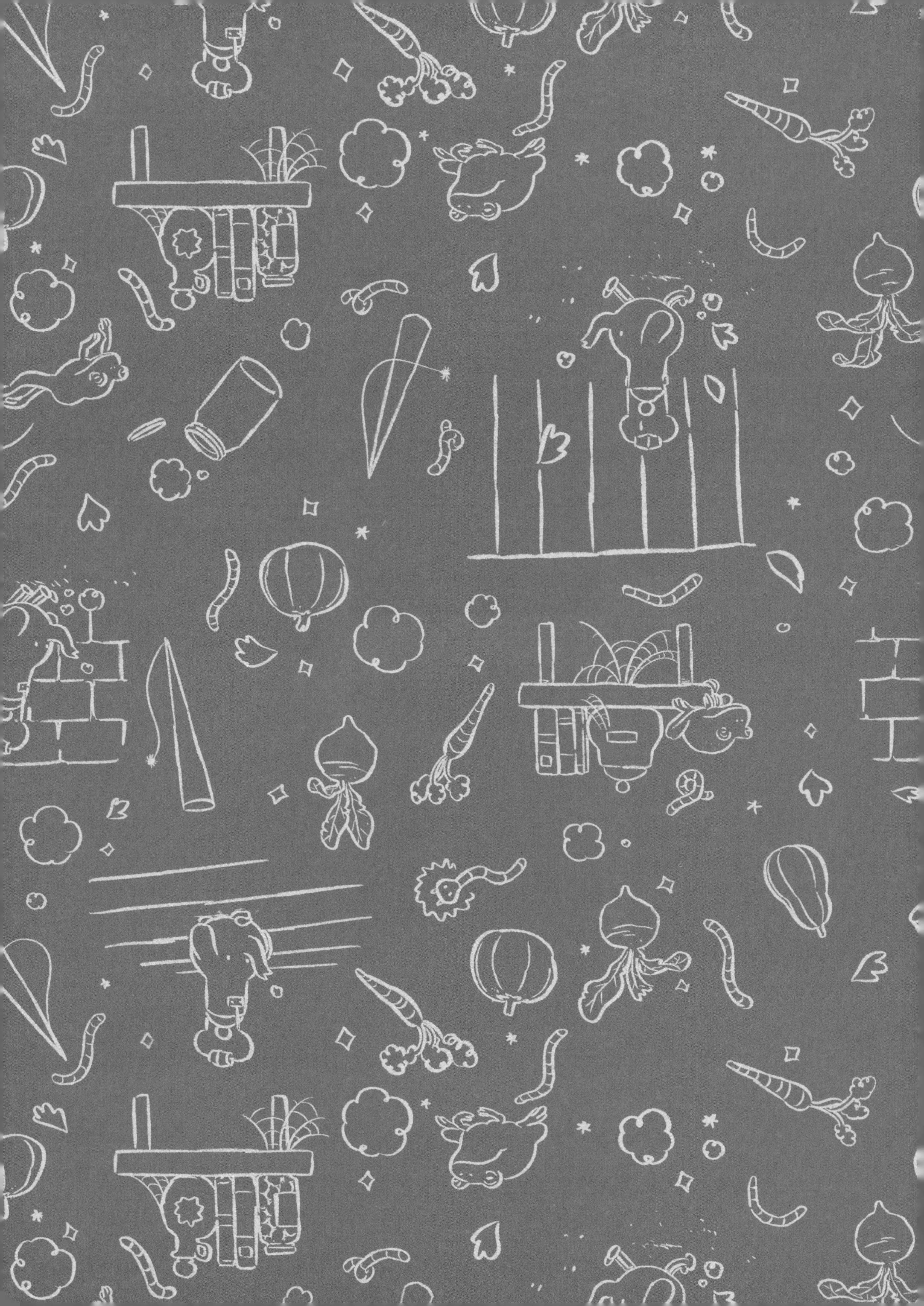

Read more exciting adventures
from Flying Eye Books...

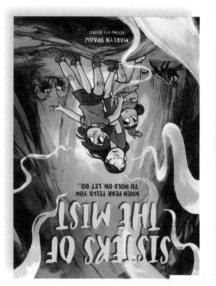

SISTERS OF
THE MIST
WHEN FEAR TELLS YOU
TO HOLD ON, LET GO...
MARLYN SPAAIJ
FLYING EYE BOOKS

NightLights
· LORENA ALVAREZ ·

SQUID HAPPENS
THE ADVENTURES OF TEAM POM
- Isabel Roxas -
flying eye books

MASON MOONEY
PARANORMAL INVESTIGATOR
SEYMOUR · MULLER
FLYING EYE BOOKS

Arthur
and the
Golden Rope
BROWNSTONE'S MYTHICAL COLLECTION
- JOE TODD-STANTON -

HILDA
AND
THE TROLL
LUKE PEARSON
FLYING EYE BOOKS

f @ ▶ 🐦 @ flyingeyebooks
www.flyingeyebooks.com